For Shaquetta and Josh
—P.C.M.

For Prisca, of course, with love.
—C.A.C.

Text copyright © 2008 by Patricia C. McKissack
Illustrations copyright © 2008 by Cozbi A. Cabrera
Introduction copyright © 2008 by Matt Arnett

Grateful acknowledgment is made to the following for permission to adapt as illustrations the following quilts: "Blocks" copyright © 1955 Aolar Mosely. Reprinted by permission of Mary Lee Bendolph. "Housetop—Twelve-Block Half-Log Cabin Variation" copyright © 1965 by Lillie Mae Pettway. Reprinted by permission of Mary Ann Pettway. "Milky Way" copyright © 1971 Nettie Young. Reprinted by permission of Nettie Young.

Visit us on the Web! www.randomhouse.com/kids
Educators and librarians, for a variety of teaching tools, visit us at
www.randomhouse.com/teachers

Library of Congress Cataloging-in-Publication Data
McKissack, Pat.
Stitchin' and pullin' : a Gee's Bend quilt / by Patricia C. McKissack ; illustrated by Cozbi Cabrera. — 1st ed.
p.   cm.
Summary: As a young African American girl pieces her first quilt together, the history of her family, community, and the struggle for justice and freedom in Gee's Bend, Alabama, unfolds.
ISBN 978-0-375-83163-8 (trade) — ISBN 978-0-375-93163-5 (lib. bdg.)
[1. Quilting—Fiction. 2. African Americans—Fiction. 3. Family life—Alabama—Fiction. 4. Alabama—Fiction.]
I. Cabrera, Cozbi A., ill. II. Title. III. Title: Stitching and pulling. IV. Title: Gee's Bend quilt.
PZ7.5.M45St 2008 [Fic]—dc22 2007011066

Book design by Roberta Ludlow

MANUFACTURED IN CHINA

10 9 8 7 6 5 4 3 2 1

First Edition

Stitchin' and Pullin'
a Gee's Bend Quilt

Patricia C. McKissack • Illustrated by Cozbi A. Cabrera

Random House New York

Acknowledgments

A special thank-you to Matt Arnett of Tinwood Alliance, who has been very supportive throughout this project. I thank you for all that you did to make this book possible. Thank you to Mr. Willie Quill, who told me the story of a special horse named Pinky, and to all the Gee's Bend citizens who treated me like a returning relative.

Thanks to my editors at Random House, Jennifer Arena and Suzy Capozzi; Cozbi for her excellent interpretation of my words; and my husband, Fredrick, and our children, without whom life would not be as full.

Introduction

Gee's Bend, in Wilcox County, Alabama, is a rural community tucked away in an isolated curve of the Alabama River. What was once a land of plantations run by white slave owners evolved after the Civil War into a society of emancipated slaves. These residents were tenant farmers who, over time, became landowners.

Set apart from the modern world, Gee's Bend has remained relatively unchanged over the years. Family, church, and traditions like quilting connect generations and continue to be the strength of the community in the twenty-first century.

Originally, quilting was the evening activity or chore of the women, which, in addition to creating covers for warmth, also gave them a platform for storytelling, communicating, and singing the songs their mothers sang. Quilting reinforced the ties between generations—from mother to daughter and beyond. Children sat beneath the quilt helping their mothers. They learned basic skills by taking the thread out of old quilts so they could be recycled for new quilts. As girls got older, they were invited to join their elders at the quilting table, where they pieced simple quilts.

Early quilts were made from materials at hand: old jeans, work clothes, and dress tails (the back of a dress, which sees the least wear and tear). Today, the quiltmakers still search through used clothing, knowing that the memory of the person who wore the shirt, pants, dress, or skirt brings special meaning to the quilt. As one of the artists (and these quiltmakers are certainly artists), Mary Lee Bendolph, says, "Those clothes have the love and spirit of the people who wore them, and that's what I want my quilts to have, love and spirit."

My family had spent the 1980s and 1990s researching and documenting the art of southern African American artists. In 1998, while doing research, we saw a breathtaking quilt in a book. A search for the quilt brought us to Gee's Bend and the surrounding towns of Rehoboth and Alberta. Our first trip to Gee's Bend revealed a world of African American art that very few people outside the region had seen. Later trips introduced us to more and more quiltmakers. We soon realized that our role was to bring to light not only the quilts but the quiltmakers as well. In doing so, we were able to share their extraordinary history and art. Through museum and gallery exhibitions, documentaries, and recordings of the sacred music of Gee's Bend—sung in the community and around the quilting frame—we've helped the world come to know these artists, their culture, and the town of Gee's Bend.

I have seen the delight in my own children's eyes during their visits to Gee's Bend. The women, their stories, and their quilts have become a part of our personal history. As Louisiana Bendolph has said many times, "We tell our stories not because we want people to feel sorry for us for what we have been through, because we don't feel sorry for ourselves. We tell our stories because we are proud of who we are and where we come from." The story woven here by Patricia McKissack's words and Cozbi Cabrera's illustrations intertwines images of actual quilts, the history of the rural South, and the fight for the rights of African Americans throughout the country, which together celebrate a significant part of our collective heritage.

Matt Arnett
December 2007

Gee's Bend Women

Gee's Bend women are
Mothers and Grandmothers
   Wives
Sisters and Daughters
   Widows.
Gee's Bend women are
Cooks and Homemakers
   Gardeners
Church members, Choir members
   Leaders.
Gee's Bend women are
Talented and Creative
   Capable
Makers of artful quilts
   Unmatched.
Gee's Bend women are
Relatives
   Neighbors
     Friends—
Same as me.

Who Would Have Thought . . .

For as long as anybody can remember,
the women of Gee's Bend
have stitched up quilts—
to be slept on and under,
sat on at a picnic,
wrapped in when sick,
or covered with while reading
on a cold winter night.

Who would have thought
that one day those same quilts
would be hanging on museum walls,
their makers famous?
Who would have ever thought?

Beneath the Quilting Frame

Baby Girl—that's me—played
beneath the quilting frame
on a "Nine Patch" quilt
my great-great-grandmother
and her sisters made
when Great-Gran
was herself Baby Girl.
I remember
the warm brown faces
of my mama, grandma, and great-gran
as they sewed, talked, sang, and laughed
above my tented playground.
All the while, steady fingers
pieced together colorful scraps
of familiar cloth
into something
more lovely
than anything they had been before.
Oh, how I remember . . .
I remember Mama's gentle voice
singing softly,
lulling her Baby Girl to sleep.

Something Else

My space beneath the quilting frame
became too small
for growing legs
and a questioning mind.
Busy
threading needles and
cutting scraps,
I listened and learned
the recipes for eleven kinds of jelly,
what to do for teething toddlers,
how to get rid of mold,
and the words to a hundred
hymns and gospel songs.
All the while
waiting for my turn.

Where to Start?

Today,
Grandma winked at me.
There is a promise in her smile.
"It is your time," she says,
"to piece your own quilt."

"How did you begin your first quilt?"
I ask Mama.
She is getting ready for work
and the long drive over to Camden.
"Look for the heart."
She pulls me close.
"When you find the heart,
your work will leap to life . . .
    strong,
        beautiful, and
            independent."

Remembering

Mama told me,
"Cloth has a memory."

I hope

the black corduroy remembers
that it was once the pants . . .
my uncle wore to go vote for the first time,
all clean and new.

I hope

the pink and green flowered tablecloth remembers
the peach cobbler
I spilled on it at the Fourth of July picnic . . .
before my brother went off to school
in Boston,
when we were still
all together.

I hope

the white lace handkerchief remembers
how pretty my cousin looked . . .
the day she got married to Junior
all over again.

I hope

the dark blue work shirt remembers
how hard Daddy has worked . . .
all his life.

If by chance the cloth forgets,
I want to always remember . . .
all of it.

Nothing Wasted

Grandma wants me to learn
to quilt using the old ways—
all by hand,
nothing wasted.

Her nut-brown hands
gently unravel the stitches
from the hem of an old red and white
gingham dress—
Stitch by stitch,
slowly she backs out of the dress,
taking apart what she'd put
together long ago.
Snip. Snip. Pull.
The thread is gone.
The dress falls apart,
a puddle of red and white gingham
on the floor.
Now I know:
A patch of Grandma's old
dress will be the heart of my quilt.

Puzzling the Pieces

A quilt
is a puzzle made of cloth—
Squares of
red and white gingham;
Solid rectangles, print ones, too;
Dotted triangles and a few plaids mixed in.
Flowered circles and long, narrow strips,
spread out on the floor.
Now comes the puzzling—
mixing and matching
colors, shapes, and patterns;
Finding combinations of pieces that
fit like a puzzle—making a picture,
telling a story.

The River Island

Grandma says her quilts tell a story,
so mine will tell one, too.
My story.

Long strips of brown cotton
border three sides of my quilt,
just as Gee's Bend
is surrounded on three sides by
brown muddy waters,
creating a river island
perfect for snakes and alligators.

A strip of green is the fourth border,
a symbol of the fields where my ancestors
worked cotton from can to can't—
can see in the morning until
can't see at night.
Years of toil on the Gee's Bend plantation,
owned by the Gee family, who lived
in a huge house called Sandy Hill.

Above the green strip I place
six squares that
form the small communities of—
   Brown Quarters
   White Quarters
   Rehoboth
   Sodom
   Over the Creek
   Lebanon
Where families with
the same name
are not kin by blood
but by plantation.

Being Discovered

A large smoke-gray square
stands for hard times,
because I've heard Great-Grandpa say,
"During the Depression of the 1930s,
bad luck and trouble hovered
over us sharecroppers
like a big ol' smothering gray hand."
Then Great-Gran adds,
"Our houses were one- or two-room shacks
with dirt floors, and
plastered in newspaper to keep out the winter wind.
Most of us didn't even
have indoor plumbing.
But it was home."

The land was poor.
My great-grandparents were poorer still.
"But we didn't know it," my mama puts in.
"We managed to be happy somehow."

Then Gee's Bend was discovered
by sociologists, historians,
educators, and journalists,
who came from everywhere.
Some to help.
Some to share.
Some to study.
Some just to see.
Photographers took hundreds of pictures.
I've seen one of Great-Gran
with Grandma, who was just a baby.

Gee's Bend got the hiccups from
all the excitement
of cameras clicking,
writers scribbling on pads,
people talking breathlessly,
never waiting for answers.
Then it was over!
Gee's Bend
took a deep breath and
went back to the way it had been
before being discovered.

Once the river ran free.
Then they built the dam
and said it was progress.

Acres and acres of rich farmland—
known as the Bottom—are flooded now.

Land
where black men and women
named Pettway and Bennett
grew cotton
before the Civil War
for no pay;

where sharecroppers
named Mingo and Williams
worked the soil
for very little pay;

and where black farmers
named Bendolph, Young, and Irby
scratched out a living
for slow pay.

Now cottonmouths, alligators, and catfish
live in the Bottom.

Call that progress?

Colors

Grandma says,
Blue cools.
Red is loud and hard to control,
like fire and a gossiping tongue.
Green oozes.
Orange laughs.
Pink smiles.
Yellow warms.
Black protects.
White shifts its shades from soft and bright to dingy.
Purple is quiet.
Lavender is sweet-smelling like a newborn baby.
Brown is hardworking.

Grandma says,
"Colors show how you
feel deep down inside."
I feel yellow right now with a hint of orange.

Stereotypes

Haven't been able to work on my quilt for two weeks.
My cousin Ashlyn's been visiting from New York City.
She left this morning. Yes!
I will miss her, maybe.
Ashlyn thinks she is as cool as blue.
She reminds me of a duck—
calm on the surface
but paddling like crazy underneath
to stay afloat.

The idea of making a quilt
was way too country for Ashlyn.
"I'd rather paint or write a poem,"
she said.
"Quilting is painting a poem with fabric,"
I told her.
Never mind.
We still did what she wanted to do.
TV,
cell phones,
CD players,
video games,
and a laptop computer with Internet hookup—
she was so surprised we have these things.
I was surprised she thought we didn't.

Pinky

Back in the 1960s,
Mr. Willie Quill broke horses
for the Alabama State Mounted Patrol.
Fine horses,
well trained.
Mr. Willie Quill knew his horses.

He knew Jimmie Lee Jackson, too.
A young man from Marion
who was shot
because he wanted to vote.
"We decided to protest the senseless killing
by marching from Selma
to the capitol in Montgomery,"
remembers Mr. Willie Quill.

"The fifty-four-mile march began in Selma
at the Edmund Pettus Bridge.
Six hundred of us stood on the bridge,
ready to march.
But the governor said no, we couldn't.
We walked anyway.
Midway the bridge,
the mounted troopers attacked.

"I remember seeing those horses,
heading straight into us. . . .
We held hands and prayed."

Beating hooves pound against the blacktop
and nightsticks hum
as the troopers swing them like lassos.
Mr. Willie Quill braces for death.
But not today. Not Bloody Sunday.
Mercifully, he sees one of his horses.
"I throwed up my arm and hollered,
'Pinky!' "
The horse broke stride and veered away,
allowing Mr. Willie Quill to live . . .
to tell the story.

Mr. Willie Quill broke horses
for the Alabama State Mounted Patrol.
Fine horses,
well trained.
Ask anybody.
Mr. Willie Quill knew his horses.
Thank goodness
Pinky knew him!

Dr. King
Brings
Hope

I stitch a patch of bright pink
to remember Pinky's story.
Next to it I sew
a spotless white patch for
the hope Dr. Martin Luther King
brought to the Bend.

I've only read about Dr. King.
Grandma saw him,
heard him,
marched with him.

On a stormy February night in 1965,
Dr. King spoke
at Pleasant Grove Baptist Church.
Grandma, with Mama in her arms,
was among the first to arrive.
Every pew was soon filled.
People stood,
some even stood outside in the rain.
With misty eyes, Grandma says,
"The words we heard that night changed our lives—
Peace, hope, justice, equality, truth, love . . . freedom!
I would have followed him anywhere."

And she did.

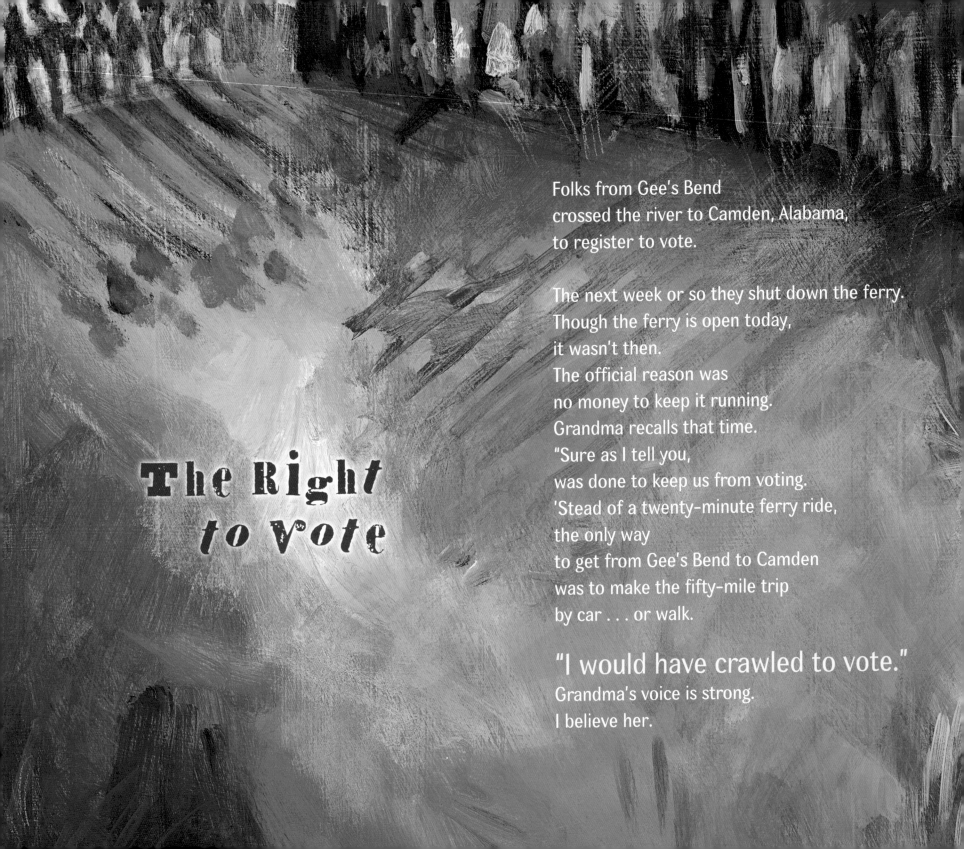

The Right to Vote

Folks from Gee's Bend
crossed the river to Camden, Alabama,
to register to vote.

The next week or so they shut down the ferry.
Though the ferry is open today,
it wasn't then.
The official reason was
no money to keep it running.
Grandma recalls that time.
"Sure as I tell you,
was done to keep us from voting.
'Stead of a twenty-minute ferry ride,
the only way
to get from Gee's Bend to Camden
was to make the fifty-mile trip
by car . . . or walk.

"I would have crawled to vote."
Grandma's voice is strong.
I believe her.

What Changed?

In 1971, the all-black school
was closed in Gee's Bend.
Black students were bused
to an all-white school fifty miles away.
Then white students went to private schools.
Today,
the once all-white school
is now mostly black.

So, what changed?

Grandma votes—no matter what!
I go to school—no matter where!
Determination is rooted in our family tree.
And that hasn't changed.

How many times have I heard
the women sing
and cry
and comfort each other
while quilting and
remembering . . . ?

So I sing, too.
I stitch a patch of golden thank-yous
for James Reeb,
a young Boston preacher
who was killed
for believing in justice.
In the background
I hear Grandma's voice softly singing,
"When the morning comes . . ."

A bright blue piece of velvet
for Viola Liuzzo,
a Detroit housewife
who also came to Gee's Bend
to help with
the big march.

Brave Viola,
wife, mother, friend—
an American Hero
assassinated.
Because she believed in justice and freedom.
Will we really understand it better
by and by?

I will mourn in a big plaid people circle
of white, black, brown, yellow, and red
for Reverend Dr. King,
who was shot
on that awful April day
in Memphis—in 1968, they say.
Will we ever understand it—
by and by?

Grandma always says that
darkness must have its hour.
But morning always comes.
Until then, we must
tell the story
of how we've overcome . . .
so we'll understand it better
by and by!

The Sewing Bee

Gee's Bend quilters were discovered again
in the 1960s.
And the Freedom Quilting Bee
was formed to make and sell quilts.
Orders came all the way from New York City.
"Were you a part of the Bee, Great-Gran?"
She closes her eyes and thinks before speaking.
"Each quilt meant
a job, some money,
a possible way out of poverty.
My children profited from it.
But with the orders
also came strict rules:
Not a stitch could be out of place.
Only traditional designs could be used—
   Nine Patch
   Wedding Ring
   Bear Claw—
Any variations were rejected!

"Yes,
more money.
Less freedom.
I chose to stay free."

My Way with Corduroy

Come the 1970s—
the Freedom Quilting Bee
began to fill orders for
Sears Roebuck.
Loads of corduroy
were sent to Gee's Bend
from Alabama textile mills.
Big bolts of it for quilting pillows . . .
bright pillows of
red, yellow, blue, and green.
Corduroy.
There is music in Great-Gran's voice
when she recalls,
"Good times came
stitching corduroy.
Great fabric for quilting
my designs.
My way.
Love that corduroy."

An Understanding Will Come Later

My quilt top is pieced.
I spread it on the bed.
Great-Gran nods her approval.
Mama smiles.
Grandma leads me to the frame
on the porch.
Knowing hands put my quilt in place.
"How long will it take?" I ask.
　　Great-Gran shushes me.
　　Come. Join us.
She holds out her hand.
Mama hums
By and by.

Five women surround me at the
quilting frame—
all stitchin' and pullin',
singing the old spirituals—
same as always, except today I am
a part of the group.

Coffee-colored,
berry-stained,
nimble fingers with clumsy thumbs,
stitchin' and pullin' . . . together

in a slow and steady rhythm . . .
patient hands that guide without force,
teach without punishment,
an old, old process,
women stitchin' and pullin'
together.

When will we finish? I ask.
Grandma's eyes
and the tilt of her head say,
Be patient—
Quilting takes time—days, even weeks.
Relax and enjoy.

I stitch and pull . . . and listen
in the warm yellow glow of an afternoon sun
on the blue quiet
of my grandma's porch.
The other women smile,
because they know.

Finished

For several days, I've been asking,
"Are we finished yet?"
Grandma laughs and her cheeks rise
in gentle mounds.
"With this one . . . last . . . stitch. . . ."

I bite the thread and knot it.
Finished.
I have made my first quilt . . .
stitchin' and pullin' . . .
with the others.

But I am not complete. . . .
There are hundreds of ideas in my head.
Quilts that are about me,
the place where I live,
and the people
who have been here for generations.

"Why are you crying, Grandma?" I ask.
"An understanding will come," she says.

"By and by," I add.

Author's Note

I first saw the exhibit of Gee's Bend quilts and learned about the women who created them at the Corcoran Gallery of Art in Washington, D.C., in 2004. I was thrilled when I was invited to write a book about them for young readers. But I had never quilted before! I had a lot of research ahead of me.

I began by reading everything I could find about African American quilt making. But it wasn't until I visited Boykin, Alabama, during the summer of 2004 that I met with the fantastic artisans of Gee's Bend and experienced quilting on a very personal level.

Mrs. Mary Lee Bendolph allowed me to stay in her home and shadow her during my weeklong visit there. I was an eager student, and Miz Mary, as I respectfully call her, was my hands-on teacher. The first thing she explained was the practical side of the craft. "My grandmother's quilts were not made to hang in a museum. We slept—our children slept—under them . . . and were kept warm," Miz Mary told me.

Quilts are found in many cultures, usually as household items, useful as well as beautiful. European colonists brought the craft of quilt making to the Americas. Africans arrived with knowledge of a form of quilting, too. Through the combination of African strip style with European patterns, new designs and techniques evolved. So did the purpose. They weren't just household items any longer, but often maps and diaries. "Freedom quilts," which originated among slaves, showed runaways a path to freedom, and "story quilts" helped those who were denied the right to read and write to keep their stories alive in fabric pictures. The women of Gee's Bend have continued the tradition of their ancestors and pushed forward with the indelible images of bold color, mixed texture, and large geometric designs for which they have become famous.

During my time in Boykin, I learned the basics of crafting a quilt, which for me was like building a textile sandwich. The top layer is usually pieced—made from colorful cloth swatches sewn in a pattern or design. The center *batting* is often made of cotton or wool, and the *backing* layer is a large sheet of fabric in a color ideally coordinated with the top. The three sections are then basted together, placed on a form, and quilted; running stitches arranged in a design hold all three layers in place. It is the top layer, the *piecing,* that makes Gee's Bend quilts unique.

Thanks to Miz Mary, I finally got my chance to stitch and pull. I felt like a kid again, being accepted within a circle of adults much like my own mother, grandmother, and aunts. Once it was known that my mother's maiden name was Petway, a common Gee's Bend surname, I was welcomed with open arms. It felt so natural for me to share my stories with them, and to sing as I pulled thread through layers of material and centuries of history.

Sometimes the women were quiet. They use quilting for self-evaluation, long-term planning, and reflection on the past. Mrs. Nettie Young explained it this way: "I take time to think things over. I can work out a problem. While my fingers are working, so is my mind—working it out."

It didn't take long for me to realize that a quilt is more than fabric and thread. A work shirt, an apron, a suit, or a dress becomes a record of a marriage, a birth, a baptism, an illness, a new house, a special event. Or the fabric might be selected because it's a historical reminder, the memory of going to vote for the first time at the age of fifty, a hurricane, the closing of the ferry to stop blacks from voting, or a visit by a prominent civil rights leader. These diary quilts are filled with the makers' personal experiences.

To be invited within the circle of handiwork is one of the oldest forms of female acceptance and companionship. Gee's Bend women are no different. Quilting has always been a bonding factor in their female relationships—mother to daughter, aunt to niece, sister to sister, grandmother to granddaughter, friend to friend. One of their rites of passage is a child's first quilt, since it's the passing of the craft from one generation to another. I was so privileged to have this experience with my newfound friends. It was also a joy to meet young girls, and a growing number of young men, who recognize that quilting is an ancient craft, yet also a fresh outlet for their creative energy and a constructive way to express their independence.

Our lives are like quilts. When all the bits and pieces of our remembered history are assembled, they become a link to the past and a beacon for future generations. Thank you for giving me the opportunity.

Patricia C. McKissack
Chesterfield, Missouri

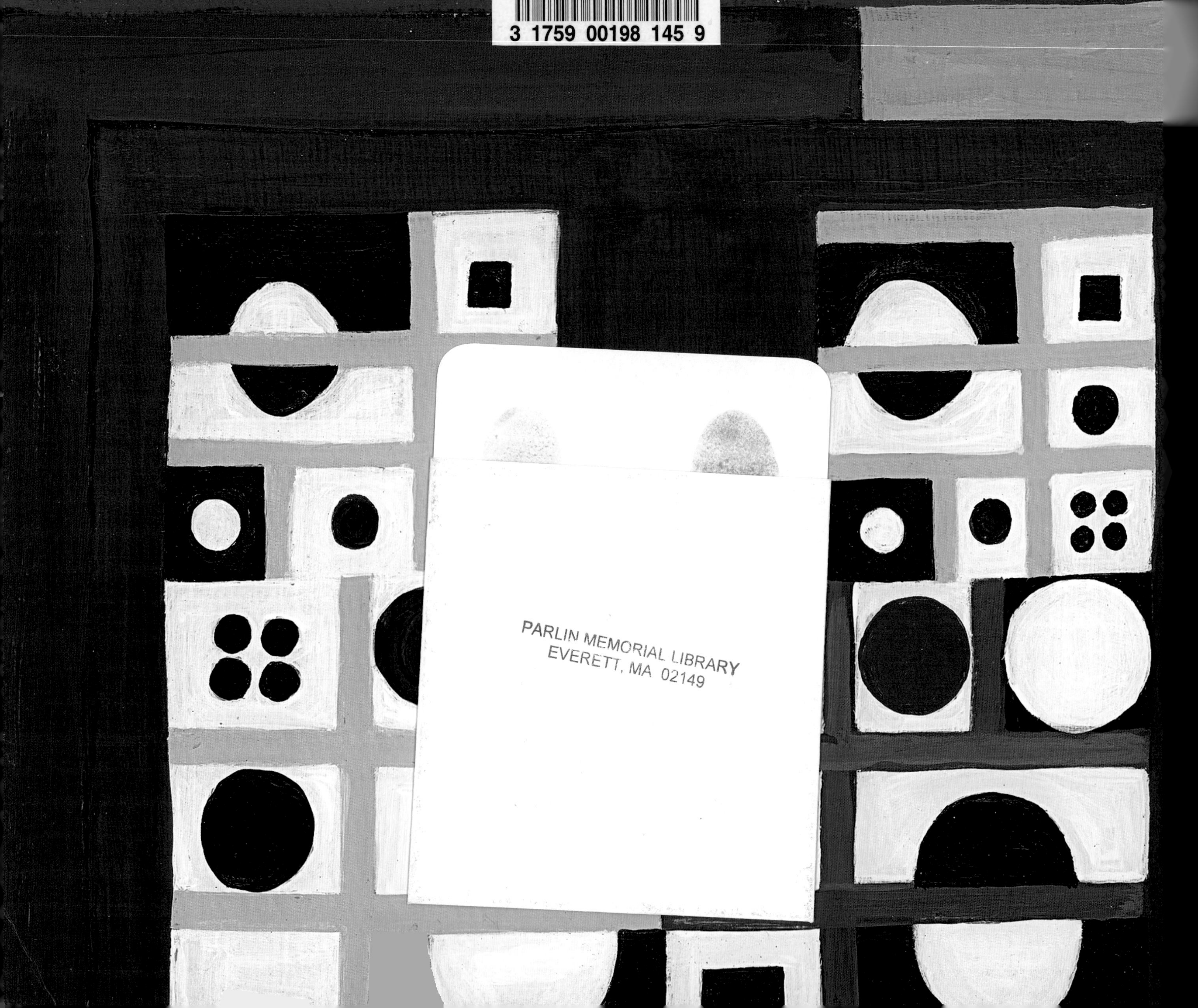